WIDGET

Lyn Rossiter McFarland   Pictures by Jim McFarland

SCHOLASTIC INC.

New York Toronto London Auckland Sydney
Mexico City New Delhi Hong Kong Buenos Aires

To Abbie, Muffin, and Widget

ISBN 0-439-46964-3

12 11 10 9 8 7 6 5 4 3 2 1   3 4 5 6 7 8/0

Printed in the U.S.A.   24

First Scholastic printing, February 2003

Typography by Judy Lanfredi

Widget was a little stray dog.
He had no home.
He had no friends.

He was very sad and lonely.
He was cold and hungry, too.

He saw a house at the end of a road.
There was a door just his size. He peeked inside.

He saw six cats,
six warm beds,
and six bowls of hot food.

Widget dove for the food—
and straight into Mrs. Diggs!

"Why, you poor thing," said Mrs. Diggs.
"I wish you could stay. But I'm afraid the girls just
can't stand dogs."

Widget looked at the girls.
He looked at Mrs. Diggs.
She seemed so nice.
Widget really wanted
   to stay.

"Meow?" said Widget.

Mrs. Diggs laughed.
"Well, girls," she said. "What do you think?"

The girls puffed up.

Widget puffed up.

The girls hissed and spit.

Widget hissed and spit.

The girls growled.

Widget purred . . . played with a toy mouse . . .
and used the litter box.

The girls stopped growling.
They were confused.
Widget looked like a dog. He smelled like a dog.
But he acted like a cat!

Mrs. Diggs set a bowl down for Widget.
Widget started eating.
He never took his eyes off the girls.

The girls started eating.
They never took their eyes off Widget.
"Why, you fit right in," said Mrs. Diggs to Widget.

And Widget did fit right in.
From that day on, Widget ran with the girls,
played with the girls, and curled up with the girls.

In fact, he had so much fun
with the girls he sometimes
forgot he was a dog!

One day, Mrs. Diggs tripped on a toy and fell down.
She didn't move.
Widget and the girls were worried.

They meowed for help.
No one came.

They screeched. They yowled.
They caterwauled for help.
No one came.

Then Widget barked for help.
The girls were shocked!

Then they barked for help, too.

Everyone came.
Mrs. Diggs was saved!

"I didn't know you had a dog," said a neighbor.
"Oh, yes," said Mrs. Diggs.
"It's nice to have a dog. Right, girls?"

Oh, yes, the girls agreed.